Anklet for a Princess

A Cinderella Story from India

Story by Lila Mehta
Adapted by Meredith Brucker
Illustrated by Youshan Tang

Library of Congress Cataloging-in-Publication Data

Brucker, Meredith Babeaux.
  Anklet for a princess : a Cinderella story from India / adapted by
Meredith Brucker ; illustrated by Youshang Tang.
      p. cm.
Summary: Cinduri, hungry and ragged, is befriended by Godfather Snake,
who feeds her delicacies and dresses her in gold cloth and anklets with
bells and diamonds, to meet the prince.
Based on a story by Lila Mehta.
  ISBN 1-885008-20-1
  [1. Folklore--India.] I. Tang, Youshang, ill. II. Title.
  PZ8.1.B832 An 2002
  398.2'0954--dc21
  Printed in China

                    2002010252

SHEN'S BOOKS
Fremont, CA

CINDURI walked slowly down the road to the lake. Her feet dragged through the dust as she balanced a heavy pot on her head. She was on her way to fetch drinking water for the family.

With a tired sigh she thought, "When I get home, I must milk the cows, clean the house, prepare yogurt and cheese for tomorrow's meals, and milk the cows again. Then I will have to clean the animal pens and pick vegetables to sell to our neighbors." Later, she knew, there would be more long trips to the lake for water for the animals.

When Cinduri arrived at the water's edge, she paused to stare out across the rippling surface. She thought of days when her life had been happier.

In those days, it was the custom in the countryside of India for a man to have more than one wife. Big families were necessary to help with the farm work. Cinduri's father had married two women, and each had a daughter. Cinduri sadly remembered the epidemic of cholera that swept through their village. Within a few days her father and mother had both died of the disease. She was left with her stepmother, a woman who cared only for her own daughter, Lata, and had no love to spare for Cinduri.

CINDURI'S eyes were shimmering with tears as she thought about how much she missed her parents. Suddenly she was startled by a showering burst of water right in front of her. She pulled back in fear as a great white snake rose up out of the lake. Her eyes were blinded by the shine of a bright red jewel on his bobbing head.

He hissed a question. "You are a beautiful young girl! Why are you so dirty and dressed in such ugly rags?"

Cinduri tried to answer politely. "There is much work to do since my father died. My stepmother and her daughter hate farm work. They like to ride to town every day in their carriage, so I am left to complete the chores."

"You do all the work for your family to maintain the farm. Why then do you look so hungry?"

"I do not need much. When my stepmother and stepsister go to feasts at the houses of friends they sometimes bring me back a little something to go with my bowl of rice."

The snake was furious. "Rice and a few handouts! That is not enough to eat!"

With a darting motion of his head, the serpent produced a golden plate. On it there was a beautiful display of East Indian foods. The almond rice, lentils, flatbread, curries, and sweet milk delights gave off tantalizing aromas. Cinduri was hungry, but before taking the plate she pressed the palms of her hands together and bowed to show her thanks to the snake.

WHEN Cinduri had finished enjoying the meal, the snake said to her, "I would like to make life easier for you from now on. Every day when you come here, I will bring you sweet fresh water from the bottom of the lake and plates of delicious food for you to eat. You will never be hungry again."

"Oh, that is wonderful," she said. "I can then use the little bowl of rice my stepmother gives me to feed the peacocks and green parrots in our garden."

"You are a good girl," he replied. "You are thankful for what you are given. And you never say one bad word about that stepmother of yours who treats you like a slave or her daughter who is so jealous of your beauty. That is why I am adopting you as my God-daughter. Now we are family, and I will do anything for you."

"You are the answer to my prayers, dear Godfather," said Cinduri, "but how will I find you again?"

The snake taught her this magic song.

> *Godfather Snake, oh Godfather Snake,*
> *Godfather Snake of the magic lake,*
> *Come to my help,*
> *For your daughter's sake!*

He told her, "Come to the lake and sing this whenever you are sad or hungry, or if you need my help."

CINDURI'S stepmother noticed a change in the girl during the following days.

"You certainly look happy and well-fed lately, Cinduri. Hurry off now and get me more of that wonderful water you have been bringing home," she ordered. She liked the water that was crystal clear, cooler and sweeter than any she had ever tasted.

As soon as Cinduri left, the old woman said to her daughter, Lata, "I want you to go after Cinduri."

"Oh, mother. It is hot today. I don't want to go outside," Lata complained.

"I don't care," her mother snapped. "You must follow that girl. Find out where she is getting such tasty water, and why she returns every day with a smile on her face."

LATA sneaked along behind Cinduri until they got to the lake. There she heard Cinduri singing.

Godfather Snake, oh Godfather Snake,
Godfather Snake of the magic lake,
Come to my help,
For your daughter's sake!

The snake appeared at once. Hiding behind a rock nearby, Lata put her hand over her mouth to stifle a terrified scream. Then Lata watched with surprise as the snake presented Cinduri a plate of delicious treats. While the girl ate, the snake disappeared under the water. Down, down he went, and reappeared with a pot filled with cool, clear water.

"Thank you, dear Godfather. This water is like a drink of the gods. And you have been kind to feed me these delicious sweets," Cinduri said, putting her hands together to bow in his direction.

Godfather Snake stared at her intently, the jewel above his eyes shining brightly.

"Cinduri, I want you to look at yourself," he commanded. "You are as beautiful as a Princess."

She looked down at her reflection in the rippling water. She saw skin as smooth as silk, eyes that curved gently into an almond shape, and lips as rosy pink as a pomegranate.

"Oh, no, Godfather," she protested. "Lata is the pretty one. My stepmother told me so."

All Grandfather Snake said in reply was, "Someday you shall see."

LATA hurried home to tell her mother what she had seen, her large ears turning pink with excitement. "Oh, the snake was frightening," she stammered. "His big shining jewel was like a third eye that could look right inside me."

The old woman began to sputter with rage. "I knew that girl had some magic in her life. The fortune tellers warned me about her. They told me she would find a way to cause us trouble."

Just then Cinduri rushed in the door, breathless. "Stepmother! Lata! I saw drummers on the road to town. A messenger was marching behind them telling everyone the news. The Crown Prince is coming to our village. He will be here on the ninth night of the Navaratri Festival!"

Each year the young people gathered at harvest time in the outdoor pavilion to meet their friends and dance for nine evenings. Cinduri was eager to attend. She hoped she might catch a glimpse of the young prince she had heard so much about.

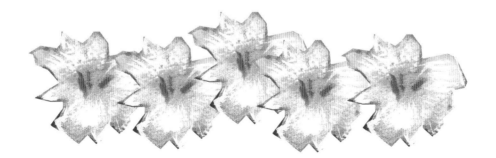

BUT when Cinduri asked permission to attend the last night of the Festival, her stepmother responded with a harsh laugh. "Oh, no. You will have to stay home and do your work."

Lata, laughing like her mother, added, "Besides, you have nothing to wear, Cinduri. You would embarrass us in those filthy rags of yours."

Cinduri huddled in a corner miserably as she watched the two women search through the family trunks. They pulled out shiny earrings, necklaces, toe rings, and belts. They draped bright veils around themselves and happily made plans for attending the Festival. Cinduri gave a tiny sob as she watched them try on the chain that had once decorated the slim ankle of her own dear mother.

At last the ninth evening of Navaratri arrived, when the aarti lamp would be lit by the visiting Crown Prince. Stepmother and Lata were dressed in all their finery. They stepped into their carriage.

Stepmother told Lata, "Maybe tonight you will meet your future husband. Or you may even meet the Prince. Pinch your cheeks. Smooth your hair." Then she glared at Cinduri and snapped, "Stop staring, Cinduri, and get back to work."

CINDURI sadly went about her household duties. After putting the last bundle of clean straw into the animal pens, she ran off toward the lake. She had to tell Godfather how much she missed going to the Festival.

When she arrived, she sang again:

Godfather Snake, oh Godfather Snake,
Godfather Snake of the magic lake,
Come to my help,
For your daughter's sake!

The snake slipped up into sight. Immediately, Cinduri told him all her troubles.

"My beautiful little God-daughter, you deserve one magical evening," he responded. He bent in her direction. "See this beautiful jewel in my forehead? Take it!" he commanded.

She obeyed him, even though the jewel felt hot to her touch.

"Don't drop it," he warned. "Now turn round and round, like this."

She watched the snake twist his body in a circle, and she copied the movements. As she slowly twirled around she felt herself being wrapped in cloth of the purest gold threads. Magnificent jewels appeared in her hair and at her throat. When she heard her feet tinkling gently, she looked down at her ankles. She saw two of the most beautiful anklets she had ever seen, decorated with tiny bells and covered with diamonds that sparkled in the moonlight.

"Go to the festival, but at midnight, when they light the candle, you must return home. The magic will be over."

"Thank you, Godfather, for this beautiful gift," Cinduri whispered as she clutched his jewel in her hands. "No matter what happens, I promise to leave at midnight."

WHEN Cinduri arrived at the Navaratri Festival, everyone turned to stare at her.

"Who is that beautiful Princess?" they all whispered.

One handsome young man asked her himself. "Who are you, beautiful Princess?" said the Prince of Suryanagar as he stepped toward her.

She looked up into his eyes but said nothing. He asked her to dance for him, and she tried to remember the flowing motions of her beloved Godfather, the snake. She twirled and dipped. The anklets jingled on her feet. The festival lights made her dark eyes shine. As she danced, the Prince watched her every motion, falling more and more in love with her with every twist and turn.

Later, everyone gathered to light the lamp for the goddess Durga, in whose honor the festival is held each year.

The Prince said to Cinduri, "It is midnight, time for the aarti. They have asked me to perform the ceremony, and I want you to join me."

"Midnight?" she gasped, as she remembered her promise to Godfather Snake. "I must go!'

She dashed away through the crowd. The Prince tried to catch her, following the sound of the bells on her feet. But she soon disappeared into the darkness.

Then he caught sight of something sparkling on the road. As he bent to pick it up, he realized it was one of her anklets. He stared into the dark night, remembering her eyes, her hair, her gentle smile. There and then, he vowed to love her forever.

THE next morning, the powerful King of Suyanagar told his son, "It is time for you to marry." He began suggesting some of the important noble ladies who could be his bride.

"But father, last night at the festival I met the one I must marry. I just don't know who she is. We have to find her," the Prince said. He pulled the tiny anklet from his pocket. "I will marry the owner of this anklet and no one else."

The King called forth messengers. He told them to go to every village. He proclaimed, "Have all the young maidens try on the anklet. The girl who can fit her foot through it will become the bride of the Crown Prince."

STEPMOTHER was very excited by the news.

She said, "The Prince will be in our village this very afternoon. Lata, you must make the anklet fit you, then the Prince will marry you. That is what the King has said!"

Cinduri asked, "May I please come with you and try on the anklet, too?"

"You? Oh, no. Lata and I will go first. You can come later, if you finish all your work," she said with a sneer. She never for a moment considered that little Cinduri, with her ragged dress and her dirty bare feet, might be the beautiful lady the Prince was looking for.

Cinduri began her chores with a hopeless feeling. There was so much to do. By the time she finished her work, the Prince would be gone. He would move on to the next town, trying the anklet on every young woman. And she would never get to tell him how much she loved him.

CINDURI hurried off to sell her vegetables to the neighbors. Then she came back to begin her sewing and mending. As her stepmother and Lata swept out the door, they reminded her that she must weed the vegetable garden in addition to all her other chores.

Cinduri knew there was no time to rush to the lake and seek the help of her Godfather, the snake. Then she remembered his magic jewel, which was hidden inside the bodice of her dress.

As soon as she cradled the bright stone in her hands, she saw miraculous changes all around her. The house was clean, the butter was churned, the weeds in the garden had disappeared, and fresh water and straw appeared in all the animal pens. Her work was all done, and her dirty dress had become clean, with not a patch on it.

"Oh, again my dear Godfather has helped me," she said, putting the jewel back in its hiding place.

As she hurried toward the pavilion she whispered over and over, "I hope I am not too late."

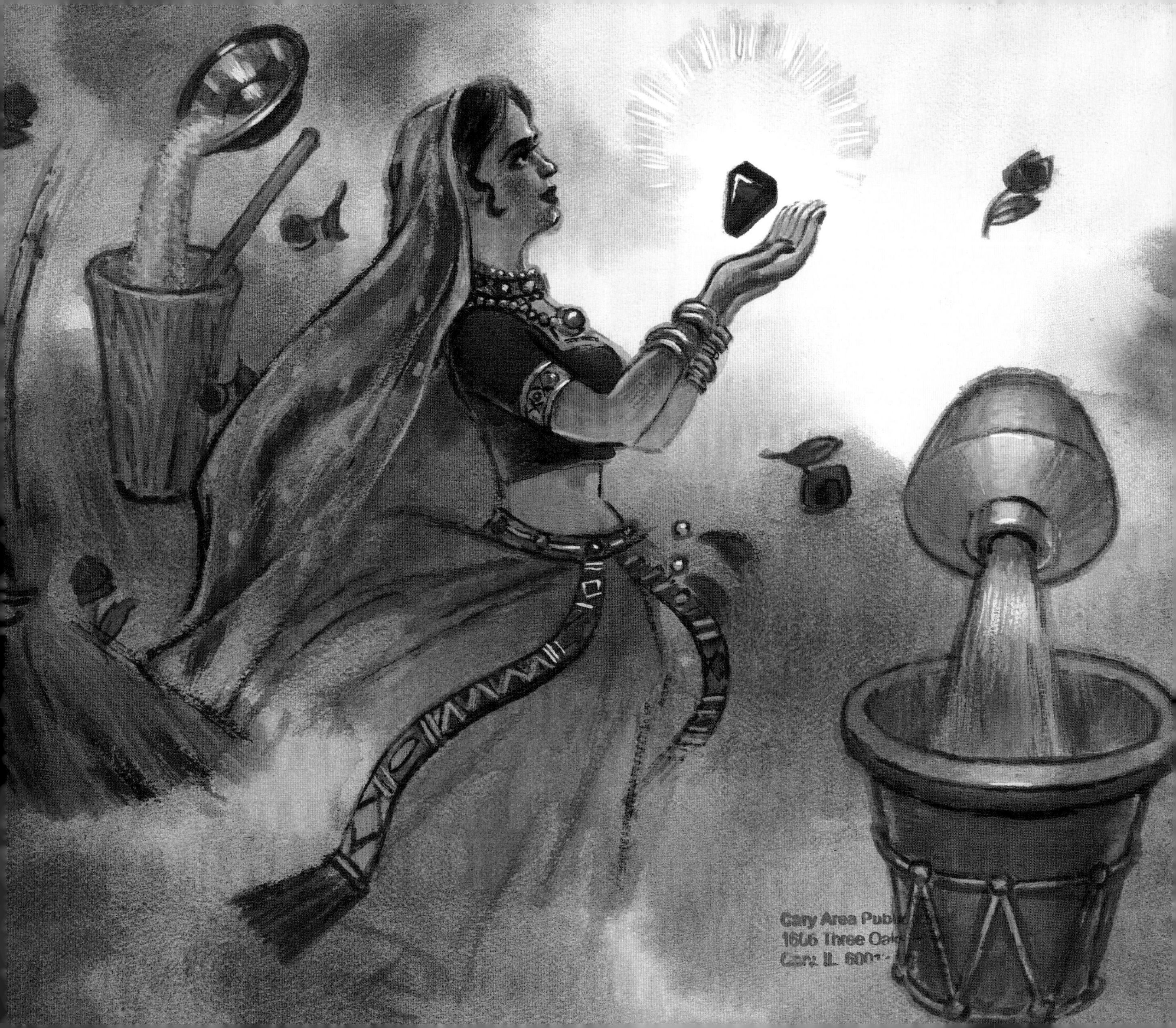

CINDURI peeked through the girls circled around the Prince. One after another they tried to squeeze their feet into the anklet.

Stepmother pulled Lata forward for her turn. The Prince knelt before her. The girl made terrible faces, trying to twist her foot through the anklet, but it was no use.

"Let us move on to the next town," said the King in a booming voice. "There I hope my son will find the woman he loves."

The Prince stood up to leave and caught sight of Cinduri.

"One more," he said, holding his hand out toward her.

Cinduri shyly moved forward.

Everyone heard Cinduri's stepmother say in a shrill voice, "What are you doing here, Cinduri? Are you sure you finished all your work? You will get a beating if you have left anything undone!"

"Quiet, everyone," ordered the Prince. "Let her try the anklet."

He slipped her foot into the jeweled circle.

There was a gasp from the crowd as Cinduri pulled from her pocket the matching anklet she had kept hidden away. This proved that she was the same girl who had danced for the Prince and won his heart.

Now, wearing both anklets, she made a slow twirling motion, as her snake Godfather had taught her.

When she finished her turn, she was standing before the people of the town dressed in the beautiful sari and all the sparkling jewelry she had worn on Festival night.

With a sparkle in his eyes that made Cinduri's heart beat wildly, the prince proclaimed, "This beautiful Princess must be my bride."

"**MR.** Prime Minister, plan a great celebration," the King announced. "The wedding will take place on the evening of the next full moon."

The King was delighted that his son had claimed such a beautiful and gentle bride. An enormous invitation was posted at the palace gates, inviting everyone in the kingdom to witness the royal wedding.

Cinduri rode to the wedding ceremony in a carriage carried on the shoulders of many servants. Walking with stately grace, she entered the special marquee built for the occasion. Inside, a fire was burning. A costumed gentleman of the court blew into a large conch shell to announce the start of the marriage ceremony.

The Prince put a garland of fragrant white jasmine flowers around Cinduri's neck, as she put one around his. They promised to love and cherish each other for the rest of their lives.

When the ceremony was over, the Prince whispered to this bride, "My father has built us a beautiful palace."

She said shyly, "I have a special friend. He is my Godfather." As she spoke, she touched the red jewel fastened on her scarf, close to her heart. "I hope I may bring him there to visit our new home."

THE Prince ordered a large pond built in the gardens of their new palace so that Godfather Snake could come to live near them and continue to bless their lives.

But he told Cinduri, "Your stepmother? Her daughter? No, no, they are not coming to live with us. I know how badly they treated you."

Once the two women had to do all their work themselves, they did it very poorly. The animals got hungry and ran away. In the garden there were more weeds than vegetables. And the house was a mess, with no fresh foods on the table.

Finally, Lata and her mother gave up on the farm and ran away to wander the countryside. Godfather Snake told Cinduri, "While they live as poor beggars, you will live for many thousands of happy days in this palace with your handsome prince. And someday you will be a loved and honored Queen."

The Princess Cinduri put her hands together in respect, bowed her head slightly, and said, "All because of you, dear Godfather. I thank you."

The End

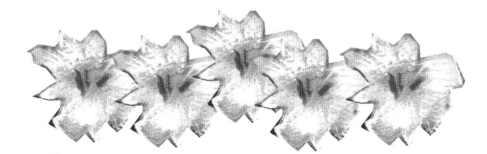

AUTHOR'S NOTE

Though this version of Cinderella set in India is very similar to the European fairy tale, it is believed that the story is at least 1,000 years old and has been preserved in oral traditions all these years.

Ancient Indian societies believed that the underwater world was a mysterious and threatening place ruled by snakes and dragons. If given offerings, these creatures would reward their benefactors with incredible fortune and good luck. Occasionally, the creature would simply take pity on an unhappy being and befriend that person.

The snake itself was a symbol of strength and might. Because its venom was used for medicinal purposes and saved lives, it was also synonymous with wealth, prosperity, and royalty. Because the snake was so revered in parts of India, many East Indian and Middle Eastern dances contain movements of a snake that reflect its importance to the culture.

LILA MEHTA was born in Rajkot, India, and graduated as a nurse and midwife in London, England. In 1965, she arrived in Canada where she graduated from the University of Toronto. She lives in Toronto with her husband and son, and teaches for the Scarborough Board of Education in Scarborough, Ontario.

MEREDITH BABEAUX BRUCKER is a graduate of Stanford University who makes her home in Southern California. She worked for many years as a writer and story editor in the TV industry — for CBS, MGM, and KTLA — and is currently employed raising public awareness of childhood cancer. A popular writing teacher, she is the author of many articles and book reviews for magazines and newspapers, and nine published novels.

YOUSHAN TANG grew up in Shanghai, China, and graduated from the Central Academy of Fine Arts and Peking University with degrees in Chinese art and literature. Since 1980, Tang has made his home in San Francisco where the cultural diversity inspires his work. He is also the illustrator of *Abadeha: The Philippine Cinderella.*